The Lost Grilled Cheese

Story by Nick E. Naro

Illustrations by Mark A. Hicks

Dedication
This one goes out to the ones I love.

On a Friday night after hockey practice, Jacky Green Bean walked into the house.

His sister, Little Lady Libby, was in the kitchen with their dad making extra cheesy grilled cheese sandwiches.

While Jacky Green Bean went upstairs to get ready for bed, his dad cooked up a storm. A storm of epic cheese.

Jacky Green Bean took a warm-glorious shower, brushed his teeth, put on cuddly-soft pajamas, and walked back to the kitchen.

Climbing up on a stool, he looked around, but all Jacky saw was an empty purple plate.

"Dad, where in the Milky Way is my grilled cheese?" asked Jacky.

"I put it on the purple plate," replied his dad.

"Um, Dad … you better sound the alarm!!!" said Jacky.

"What alarm?"

"The one that goes off when a grilled cheese is missing!" said Jacky.

"Oh, well okay. RREEAARR-REAR-RREEAARR-REAR!" His dad did his best emergency siren sound. "Let's get that sandwich back, son. What is your plan?!"

With no time to respond, Jacky Green Bean ran off to his room.

Jacky Green Bean decided he would search the world over for his grilled cheese.

Jacky gathered supplies and packed his bag with a hat, binoculars, and flashlight.

"It is time for me to hit the road," he said. "Or, is it high time for me to get to sea?" Jacky thought, smiling.

He grabbed his bag of supplies and headed to the nearest sea-port to find a Captain.

Jacky Green Bean found a Captain and started the journey to find his missing sandwich.

He was headed to Africa with Captain Jelly Surfer on an old wooden ship.

Out at sea, Captain Jelly Surfer asked about the lost cheesy sandwich.

"It is crispy brown all around, and is warm to the touch," Jacky stated.

"When you hold it with two hands it pours out a soft, shiny, golden treasure," said Jacky, smiling.

"Aye, me little man be searchin' for a treasure!" said Captain Jelly Surfer.

"Where do you think would be a good place to look for my cheesy golden treasure?" asked Jacky.

Captain Jelly Surfer was so excited by the word treasure that he thought the missing grilled cheese was a real treasure chest filled with gold!

"Well, if I were he and he were I, he would tell I to hop a ride on an elephant's hide. The elephant will race a fast while up to the River Nile," said the Captain.

"Oh boy!" shouted Jacky Green Bean. "But where will we stop?" he asked.

"Yaarr, it be in Egypt me little man may find his prize. That is if I were he and had two eyes!" said Captain Jelly Surfer, chuckling.

The ship arrived off the coast of Africa. Jacky grabbed his bag, jumped ship and made his way to shore.

He didn't have to wander far as he found that friendly elephant ride, just as the Captain had said.

Jacky Green Bean hopped on the friendly elephant and away they rode.

Jacky waved good-bye, "Thank you! Thank you Captain Jelly Surfer!"

The friendly elephant ran like the wind.

They arrived in Egypt and Jacky searched the pyramids high and low, but he found no treasure and found no grilled cheese.

He searched the Sphinx. He asked many mummies, but no lost grilled cheese.

He could hear his stomach start to growl and decided to move on and keep searching.

Jacky Green Bean decided to see if the King of Egypt could offer any help.

"Hello, Mister Pharaoh! Could you help me find my lost grilled cheese?" asked Jacky.

"Please, call me Daddio," replied the Pharaoh.

"Okay, Mister Daddio. I really need to find this grilled cheese before I go to bed, can you help me?" asked Jacky.

"Why of course, my young Prince," responded the King of Egypt.

"But, if the famous cheese that you speak of is what you seek, it shall be far from here."

The Pharaoh continued, "If for the lost grilled cheese you so desperately care, then I have this special camel that you can ride and her secret I shall share!"

The Pharaoh confessed, "She is an extraordinary beast. She cannot walk or run in the least, but son, she can fly!"

So, with that and without hesitation, Jacky Green Bean mounted the special camel beast.

Jacky held on tightly, she spread her wings, and toward Mount Everest they flew!

Thank goodness the flying special camel was able to land on top of Mount Everest, because Jacky never would have been able to climb it alone!

There he stood on top of the mountain. He peered to the left and he peered to the right, but the extra cheesy grilled treat was nowhere to be seen.

From atop the world it seemed that Jacky would never find his golden cheese treasure.

As he was putting away his binoculars, Jacky saw what looked like the Statue of Liberty.

She was running with one hand carrying her torch and the other one holding the lost grilled cheese!

Jacky grabbed a sled and flew down the mountain, racing after the Statue of Liberty!

He followed her around Mount Everest.

Past the Pyramids of Egypt he chased after her.

"Daddio! I found the treasure!" he shouted.

Jacky ran at her heels through Africa past the friendly elephant.

He waved to Captain Jelly Surfer as they swam across the big blue sea!

"Aye-Aye, Captain! I've found the treasure!" he yelled out.

Jacky Green Bean traveled the world for his lost grilled cheese sandwich, and he caught up with the Statue of Liberty at the kitchen table.

"Hello, young Prince," said Pharaoh Daddio. "I have something to give you for all of your travels."

The Pharaoh handed him a warm and especially cheesy grilled cheese sandwich.

He was so happy as he bit into the golden cheese treasure.

"You know what?" said Jacky, laughing. "Next time my sandwich goes missing, I'll know where to look."

The Statue of Liberty started laughing as they each finished a grilled cheese sandwich before going to bed.

94523050R00022